Ride, Sally Ride

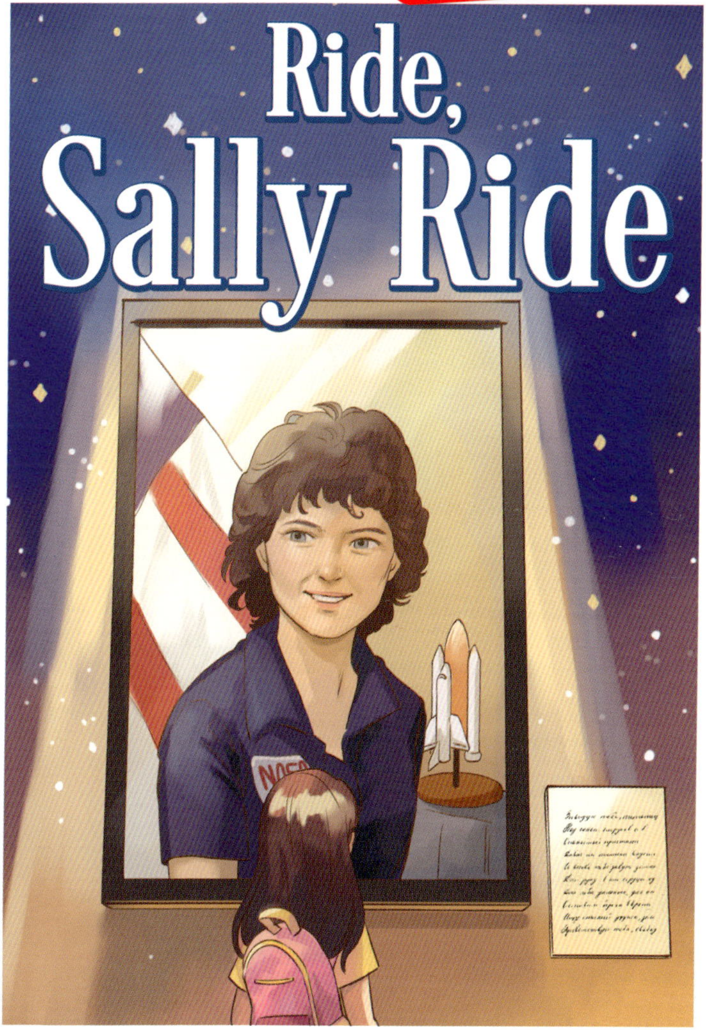

By Caroline Tung Richmond
Illustrated by Felia Hanakata

Consultant
  Kristin Risdahl, M.S.Ed.
  K–12 Social Studies Instructional Facilitator
  Knox County Schools, Tennessee

Publishing Credits
  Rachelle Cracchiolo, M.S.Ed., *Publisher*
  Emily R. Smith, M.A.Ed., *VP of Content Development*
  Véronique Bos, *Creative Director*
  Dani Neiley, *Associate Editor*
  Kevin Pham, *Graphic Designer*

Image Credits
Illustrated by Felia Hanakata

Library of Congress Cataloging-in-Publication Data
Names: Richmond, Caroline Tung, author. | Hanakata, Felia, illustrator.
Title: Ride, Sally Ride / by Caroline Tung Richmond ; illustrated by Felia Hanakata.
Description: Huntington Beach, CA : Teacher Created Materials, [2022] | Audience: Grades 2-3. | Summary: "Nine-year-old Aimee dreams about becoming an astronaut, just like her hero Sally Ride. She can't wait to visit the space museum and compete for a neat prize. But can she beat the smartest kid in her class to win it?"-- Provided by publisher.
Identifiers: LCCN 2022005942 (print) | LCCN 2022005943 (ebook) | ISBN 9781087605432 (paperback) | ISBN 9781087632292 (ebook)
Subjects: LCSH: Readers (Primary) | LCGFT: Readers (Publications)
Classification: LCC PE1119.2 .R547 2022 (print) | LCC PE1119.2 (ebook) | DDC 428.6/2--dc23/eng/20220215
LC record available at https://lccn.loc.gov/2022005942
LC ebook record available at https://lccn.loc.gov/2022005943

5482 Argosy Avenue
Huntington Beach, CA 92649
www.tcmpub.com

ISBN 978-1-0876-0543-2
© 2023 Teacher Created Materials, Inc.
Printed in Malaysia.THU001.50393

This book may not be reproduced or distributed in any way without prior written consent from the publisher.

Table of Contents

Chapter One:
   The Announcement................4

Chapter Two:
   The Contest....................10

Chapter Three:
   The Field Trip.................16

Chapter Four:
   The Winner 22

Chapter Five:
   The Prize......................28

About Us..........................32

Chapter One

THE ANNOUNCEMENT

"Listen up, class! Let's talk about our field trip tomorrow," Ms. Perez said from the front of the room.

Aimee sat up straight in her seat while her classmates yawned. It was Monday morning, but she felt wide-awake. She couldn't wait to visit the space museum.

"To prepare for the visit, we're holding a contest called the Astronaut Challenge," Ms. Perez went on. "It'll have three events. The student with the highest total score will get a special prize."

Aimee scooted to the edge of her chair. What could the prize be?

"The winner will have lunch with an astronaut during the field trip!" Ms. Perez exclaimed.

Aimee's mouth fell open. Ever since she was a little girl, she'd wanted to become an astronaut like her hero, Sally Ride. Back in 1983, Sally became the first woman from the United States to fly into space. And one day, Aimee hoped to become the first Chinese American woman in space. Now she had the chance to meet a real-life space explorer.

But she wasn't the only one who wanted to win. Across the room, a girl named Ivy raised her hand.

"Can we take a picture with the astronaut, Ms. Perez?" Ivy asked.

Ms. Perez had a glint in her eye, like a twinkling star. "You can—if you win."

Aimee felt a flutter in her stomach. Ivy was the smartest kid in their class. How could Aimee ever beat her? But then she thought about Sally Ride. When Sally was young, there had been no women astronauts at all. She had to work very hard to become one of the first.

That's what I have to do, Aimee thought. *I have to try my best to win.*

Chapter Two

THE CONTEST

Ms. Perez led the students onto the blacktop. "Ready for our first event, everyone?"

"I'm ready!" Ivy said.

"Me, too!" Aimee said a second later.

Ms. Perez asked the class to line up at the end of the blacktop. "Astronauts have to study hard, but they also need to be healthy and strong to live in space. So for our first event, you'll be running a race. The winner will get the most points."

Aimee squinted toward the finish line, which looked pretty far off. *You're fast*, she reminded herself. She took tennis lessons every week, just like Sally did growing up in California. Sally even thought about playing tennis as a career, but she'd wanted to become a scientist more.

"On your mark," Ms. Perez called out. "Get set…go!"

Aimee took off sprinting, quick as a comet. But right before she crossed the finish line, Ivy zoomed past her.

"Ivy wins!" Ms. Perez said. "Aimee comes in second."

Aimee groaned—she had gotten so close! But Ivy beat her by inches. She would have to try harder during the next round.

Back in the classroom, Ms. Perez explained their second event. "Up in space, astronauts use robotic arms to move supplies. For our second event, we're creating arms to help us complete a task."

The students used wooden craft sticks and pins to make the arms. Then, Ms. Perez placed a bunch of table-tennis balls on the floor. "Now, use the arms you made to pick up as many balls as you can. You'll have two minutes."

Aimee couldn't wait to begin. This was her chance to be like Sally, who had been the first woman to use the robotic arm on the space shuttle.

Ms. Perez counted down. "Three…two…one…go!"

The kids raced around the room, reaching for the balls but dropping them. Aimee moved slower, holding each ball tightly so it wouldn't fall.

When the two minutes were up, Ms. Perez tallied the scores. "It looks like Aimee won with six total!"

Aimee's classmates gave her high-fives, but she knew that her points and Ivy's points were neck and neck. She would have to try her best to win the last round.

Chapter Three

THE FIELD TRIP

The day of the field trip had arrived.

The students boarded a school bus and rode downtown to the museum. Aimee walked into the building with her heart racing, fast as a rocket. Above her head, she saw a model of the solar system hanging from the ceiling. Next to planet Earth, she noticed a white-and-black spaceship. She smiled. It was a model of the space shuttle *Challenger*, the same one Sally had ridden on her two missions.

"Does everyone have their papers and pencils?" Ms. Perez asked.

"I do!" Aimee said.

"Same here!" Ivy chimed in.

"Remember, you have one hour to finish your assignment. Meet me here at noon, and don't be late or you won't get any points."

Aimee hurried off. In the *Stargazing* exhibit, she sketched the parts of a telescope. In the Planets and Moons room, she wrote how many moons each planet had. Then, she tackled the questions about astronauts. She felt excited that she knew most of the answers already.

Where do NASA astronauts train? Aimee knew that they trained in Houston, Texas. That was where Sally did her training.

How do astronauts talk to people on Earth? Aimee wrote that they used radios, like the ones Sally learned how to use.

Aimee glanced at her watch and yelped. It was 11:57 a.m. already! She leapt onto her feet, but on her way out of the exhibit, she noticed Ivy was still finishing her assignment. If Ivy didn't leave right now, she wouldn't get any points at all, which meant Aimee would probably win the Astronaut Challenge.

Aimee hesitated. She really wanted to have lunch with the astronaut, but she knew deep down she didn't want to win this way.

"Ivy!" she called out. "We better go."

Ivy looked up. "Whew, thanks! I didn't know we were almost out of time."

The two girls raced to the entrance. "Here you go, Ms. Perez," they said, handing in their papers.

"Perfect timing. You two got here just in time," Ms. Perez said. The class surrounded their teacher, like planets orbiting a star. "Let me tally the points, and I'll announce the winner soon."

Aimee crossed her fingers. Would she have enough points to get first place?

Chapter Four

THE WINNER

"The top two scores were very close. But the winner is..." Ms. Perez trailed off.

Aimee held her breath. *Let it be me,* she thought. *Please, let it be me.*

Ms. Perez pointed at the winner. "Ivy!"

The rest of the students cheered while Ivy beamed like a new star. Aimee managed a smile, even though her heart felt like it had sank into her stomach.

Ms. Perez clapped. "While I escort Ivy upstairs, the chaperones will take everyone else to the cafeteria. We'll keep exploring the museum after lunch."

The kids formed a line for lunch, but Aimee lingered behind. She knew she should stick close to her class, but she wasn't hungry. She just wanted to be alone.

Shoulders slumped, she wandered into a nearby exhibit. Paintings hung on the walls in a galaxy of colors, but Aimee barely saw them. Her eyes filled with tears. She had tried so hard to get first place, but she still missed out on meeting an astronaut.

Aimee wiped the tears away. She'd better find her classmates before she got in trouble, but when she looked up, something caught her eye. It was a portrait of a woman with brown curly hair.

It was Sally Ride.

Aimee walked up to the painting. Ever since she was five years old, she had wanted to be like Sally, but now she wasn't so sure she could.

"If I couldn't even win the challenge, how can I ever become an astronaut?" Aimee whispered to Sally's portrait.

The painting, of course, stayed silent. Aimee sighed.

"I guess I better go," she said to the empty room.

Chapter Five

THE PRIZE

But Aimee dragged her feet. She didn't feel ready to talk to anyone yet, so she let her eyes drift toward the little sign next to the painting. It described Sally's childhood before her astronaut training.

NASA selected Sally for the shuttle program in 1978, but she didn't go into space until 1983. During those five years, she took many classes and learned how to live in space. She also worked on the shuttle's ground crew, Aimee read to herself.

"Wow," Aimee whispered. She hadn't known that it had taken Sally five years to train. It must have been hard, and she might have wanted to quit, but she had pushed through it. She hadn't given up.

If I want to be like Sally, Aimee thought, *then I can't give up either. Especially when I'm feeling down.*

Just then, Aimee heard someone calling her name. She turned around to see Ivy jogging toward her.

"I've been looking for you," Ivy said, stopping to catch her breath.

"What's wrong?" Aimee asked, confused. Ivy had left for lunch only a few minutes earlier.

"Nothing! We actually have one more seat open at lunch, and Ms. Perez said I could invite anyone I wanted." Ivy started to smile. "Do you want to come?"

Aimee blinked. "You want me to eat lunch with you *and the astronaut*?"

"You don't have to say yes, but I thought—"

"Are you kidding? I'd love to go!" Aimee said, beaming.

Ivy laughed. "That's great because they're waiting for us upstairs."

Aimee started to follow Ivy down the hallway but stopped short. "Wait a second! I, um, forgot something," she said.

She dashed back to the portrait and stared up into Sally's eyes, wishing she could hug the painting. "I'm going to work really hard, and I'm not going to give up," Aimee said quietly.

Then, she ran to join Ivy. Aimee was ready for lunch and even more ready to race to the stars, just like Sally Ride.

About Us

The Author
Caroline Tung Richmond has always loved space. She even worked at a museum just like the one Aimee visits. Now, she writes books for kids—about space! Learn more about Caroline at carolinetrichmond.com.

The Illustrator
Felia Hanakata is an illustrator and comic artist based in Indonesia where there is a lot of sun and rain. She believes storytelling breathes life and colors into the world. When she is not drawing, she reads, drinks lots of coffee, plays video games, and looks for inspiration in nature and her surroundings. You can find her online at feliahanakata.com.